Dear Parents:

Congratulations! Your child is taking the first steps on an exciting journey. The destination? Independent reading!

STEP INTO READING® will help your child get there. The program offers five steps to reading success. Each step includes fun stories and colorful art or photographs. In addition to original fiction and books with favorite characters, there are Step into Reading Non-Fiction Readers, Phonics Readers and Boxed Sets, Sticker Readers, and Comic Readers—a complete literacy program with something to interest every child.

Learning to Read, Step by Step!

Ready to Read   Preschool–Kindergarten
• big type and easy words • rhyme and rhythm • picture clues
For children who know the alphabet and are eager to begin reading.

Reading with Help   Preschool–Grade 1
• basic vocabulary • short sentences • simple stories
For children who recognize familiar words and sound out new words with help.

Reading on Your Own   Grades 1–3
• engaging characters • easy-to-follow plots • popular topics
For children who are ready to read on their own.

Reading Paragraphs   Grades 2–3
• challenging vocabulary • short paragraphs • exciting stories
For newly independent readers who read simple sentences with confidence.

Ready for Chapters   Grades 2–4
• chapters • longer paragraphs • full-color art
For children who want to take the plunge into chapter books but still like colorful pictures.

STEP INTO READING® is designed to give every child a successful reading experience. The grade levels are only guides; children will progress through the steps at their own speed, developing confidence in their reading.

Remember, a lifetime love of reading starts with a single step!

For Elise
—E.B.
For Pepper
—E.G.

The Nez Perce words that appear in Kaya's story are spelled so that English readers can pronounce them.

Nimíipuu (nee-MEE-poo) means **the People** (known today as the Nez Perce)

Eetsa (EET-sah) means **mother**

Toe-ta (TOH-tah) means **father**

Aalah (AA-lah) means **grandmother** (on father's side)

All rights reserved. Published in the United States by Random House Children's Books, a division of Penguin Random House LLC, 1745 Broadway, New York, NY 10019, and in Canada by Penguin Random House Canada Limited, Toronto.

Step into Reading, Random House, and the Random House colophon are registered trademarks of Penguin Random House LLC.

Visit us on the web!
StepIntoReading.com
rhcbooks.com

Educators and librarians, for a variety of teaching tools, visit us at RHTeachersLibrarians.com

ISBN 978-0-593-48328-2 (trade)—ISBN 978-0-593-48329-9 (lib. bdg.)
ISBN 978-0-593-48330-5 (ebook)

Printed in the United States of America
10 9 8 7 6 5 4 3 2 1

☆ American Girl®

Kaya

Rides to the Rescue

by Emma Carlson Berne

illustrated by Emma Gillette

Based on a story by Janet Shaw

Random House 🏠 New York

Kaya rides into the river valley.

The sun sparkles on the water.

Kaya's family has come to fish
for salmon.

The year is 1764.

Kaya is part of the
Nimíipuu people—the Nez Perce.

Kaya loves nature and
the beauty of this special place.

She has a horse named Steps High.

She loves to ride fast!

Kaya has a special bond
with her horse.
Steps High comes
when Kaya whistles.
Kaya's best friend is
Speaking Rain.
Speaking Rain is blind.
Kaya and Steps High
gently lead Speaking Rain
on her horse.

Speaking Rain lives with
Kaya's family. Kaya and
Speaking Rain are like sisters.
Brown Deer is Kaya's big sister.

Kaya helps take care of
her twin brothers,
Wing Feather and Sparrow.
They love to hide, and
sometimes, they don't listen.
Kaya's mother, Eetsa, often
asks Kaya to watch the boys.

Kaya's grandmother, Aalah,
is waiting to welcome the family
when they ride up.
Kaya's father, Toe-ta,
her sister Brown Deer,
and the others
help untie the bundles and
bring them into the tepee.

Eetsa says Kaya and Speaking Rain

can take the twins to play.

She reminds Kaya to watch them.

Kaya promises she will.

A boy named Fox Tail
teases Kaya. He says Steps High
is not very fast. Kaya boasts
that Steps High is fast.
"She's as fast as an eagle!"
Kaya says.
"Let's race!" Fox Tail replies.
Kaya asks Speaking Rain
to take care of the twins,
even though that's Kaya's job.

The horse race is on!

Kaya is worried.

Steps High has not raced before.

Kaya wishes she hadn't boasted.

The horses leap forward.

Kaya pushes Steps High to go

faster and faster. Suddenly,

Steps High rears and bucks!

Kaya slides off and calms Steps High.

She knows it was wrong

to race her young horse.

Still, Kaya wishes she had won.

She challenges Fox Tail

to a race on foot.

Fox Tail runs far ahead.

Kaya is alone. She is not sure

which way to go.

She hears birds caw.

They seem to say, "Forgot! Forgot!"

Then Kaya remembers the twins!

She promised Eetsa to watch them.

Kaya runs back toward the river

as fast as she can.

Speaking Rain sits by the river.

She tells Kaya that the boys

ran away from her.

Now she can't find them.

Kaya's heart pounds.

They could fall into the river!

Kaya and Speaking Rain

search along the river and in the woods.

They find the boys up in a tree.

The boys are safe, but Kaya's auntie

saw what happened.

Kaya is in trouble.

Kaya was selfish, Auntie says.

She forgot her brothers,

so all the children

will be punished.

This will remind them

that what one person does

affects everyone.

Fox Tail calls Kaya "Magpie,"

after the selfish bird that

snatches what it wants.

It thinks only of itself.

While making dinner, Kaya tells
Aalah about her mistake. How can
she lose her awful nickname, Magpie?
Kaya should think of her brothers'
safety before her own fun,
Aalah says. She can work
with Steps High to earn the trust
of her horse and family again.
Maybe then, she will lose her nickname.

In the morning, Kaya and Toe-ta
train Steps High.
Kaya is calm and quiet,
so Steps High stays
calm and quiet as well.

Fox Tail rides up to Kaya.

He wants to race again.

This time, Kaya says no.

Steps High is not ready to race.

Fox Tail calls her Magpie

and rides off!

Kaya trains Steps High each day.

She teaches Steps High

to trust her.

She thinks about her nickname

and what she must do to get rid of it.

The salmon-fishing season ends.

The family is packing up.

Aalah can't find her special knife.

Kaya offers to look for it

near the riverbank.

Speaking Rain comes, too.

Speaking Rain says she will
search along the bushes.
Kaya searches farther downstream.
Speaking Rain moves too close
to the riverbank.
Suddenly, Kaya sees Speaking Rain
tumble into the river!

Kaya gallops Steps High

along the river.

Speaking Rain is struggling

in the rushing water.

Kaya must reach her.

"Trust me," she tells her horse.

Steps High wades into the water.

Kaya reaches Speaking Rain.

She pulls her onto Steps High.

They return to the riverbank, safe.

Toe-ta helps Speaking Rain

off the horse. He saw what happened.

Toe-ta tells Kaya she did well.

She earned Steps High's trust.

She raced to help Speaking Rain,

instead of racing to win.

"Good job, Kaya," says Fox Tail.

He calls Kaya by her name,

instead of Magpie.

Kaya hugs Steps High.

"Thank you," she whispers.

Kaya's family leaves the valley.

She rides Steps High out

to help herd the other horses.

She is proud to do her work

for her people.

Kaya will not be Magpie anymore!